The TiNKLERS THREE

A Very Good Idea
published in 2014 by
Hardie Grant Egmont
Ground Floor, Building 1, 658 Church Street
Richmond, Victoria 3121, Australia
www.hardiegrantegmont.com.au

A CiP record for this title is available from the National Library of Australia.

Text copyright © 2014 MC Badger
Illustration copyright © 2014 Leigh Brown
Series design copyright © 2014 Hardie Grant Egmont

Design by Elissa Webb
Illustrations by Leigh Brown

Printed in Australia by Griffin Press, an Accredited ISO AS/NZS
14001:2004 Environmental Management System printer.

1 3 5 7 9 10 8 6 4 2

The TINKLERS THREE

a VERY good IDEA

M·C·BADGER

illustrated by
leigh brown

hardie grant EGMONT

CHAPTER ONE

MARCUS TINKLER lived with his two sisters, Mila and Turtle, in their flat on the thirty-third floor of number thirty-three, Rushby Road.

Marcus's big sister, Mila, was full of ideas. Every time Mila sneezed, she got a new idea. Some of Mila's ideas were good. Some were not so good.

This was one of Mila's good ideas:

The BEST food for BREAKFAST is CHOCOLATE ice-cream.

This was a not-so-good idea:

A bird's NEST makes a GOOD hat.

(She thought the hat was even better if there was a bird living in it.)

Marcus's younger sister was called Turtle. Why was she called that? Because she thought she was a turtle. She had never seen a real turtle. But this is what she knew about them: They have shells. They eat lettuce. They growl. They like sticks.

Marcus thought that he was definitely the most normal of the three Tinklers.

Maybe you think he was right. But let me tell you a secret. Come closer to the book so I can say it quietly:

MARCUS was NoT REALLY that NORMAL.

None of the Tinklers were.

For one thing, the Tinkler children lived all alone in their flat on the thirty-third floor of thirty-three Rushby Road.

The Tinklers lived alone because their parents worked in a travelling circus. Their father was a tightrope walker, and their mother rode a white horse. But she didn't sit down in the saddle like a normal person would. Oh no. She stood up on the horse's back and twirled like a ballerina, with one leg in the air.

When the Tinkler children were older, they could join the circus too.

But for now they lived by themselves. This meant that the Tinklers Three got to do things their own way.

* * *

One morning Marcus woke up with a dream stuck in his head. As I'm sure you know, most dreams turn into dust the moment you open your eyes.

The dust comes out of your ears and falls to the ground. This is why it gets so dusty under your bed. At least, that's what Mila said.

But this particular morning, Marcus's dream stayed inside his head and turned into a question instead. It was this:

CAN I get from MY BED to the DOORWAY without ONCE touching the GROUND?

Marcus sat up in his bed and looked down at the floor below.

He and Mila had always wanted bunk beds. But they both wanted to sleep on the top bunk. Luckily, Mila sneezed and had a great idea. It was this:

Why not take two NORMAL beds and nail them BOTH to the wall UP HIGH?

That way they could *both* have a top bunk, and nobody would have to sleep on the boring old bottom bunk.

Mila was still asleep on her bunk. This was no surprise. Mila always slept in.

Turtle didn't sleep in a bed. She slept in a green cardboard box. She said this was one of her shells.

Now, everyone knows that turtles only have one shell. And they can't get out of their shells whenever they want to. But if you said this to Turtle she would growl at you. She might even nip your toes.

Marcus saw that Turtle's shell was empty. This was also no surprise. Turtle always woke up very early. She liked to crawl into the lounge room to play with her stick collection.

Marcus pulled off his covers and wriggled to the edge of his bed. He was sure he could make it to the door without touching the ground.

Not far below was a chest of drawers. The Tinklers didn't keep their clothes in drawers. Mila said that clothes should be kept on the floor where they were easy to find.

The chest was very sturdy. Marcus was sure it would hold his weight.

He dangled his feet out over the edge of his bed and then jumped down. *Easy!*

The next step was getting onto the bookshelf. This was not so easy.

Maybe you think that the bookshelf was a shelf FOR books. Wrong. It was a shelf MADE OF books.

Marcus knew the books might slip and slide away when he landed on  them. So he was very careful as he put his feet down.

The bookshelf WOBBLED...

The bookshelf ROCKED...

But it did not fall.

Slowly, Marcus shuffled across the top of the books.

Hmm . . . the bedroom door was still a long way away, and there were no more bookshelves or chests of drawers left for Marcus to use. Maybe this idea wouldn't work after all.

But then Marcus spied the mini-trampoline in the middle of the room. He had forgotten about it because it was usually covered with clothes. Marcus and Mila used the trampoline to get up onto their beds. It was just what he needed!

Marcus crouched on the edge of the bookshelf. Then he took a huge jump onto the mini-trampoline.

He bounced up in the air and grabbed hold of the light above him. The light cord was made from a bit of leftover tightrope so it was very strong. It was also very swingy.

Marcus used the cord to swing across to the door frame.

Yes! He had done it.

Then Marcus heard a sleepy voice behind him. 'What are you doing?'

He swung around and saw Mila sitting up in her bed, rubbing her eyes.

'I made it from my bed to the door without touching the ground,' said Marcus.

'That's a very good idea,' said Mila. 'It sounds like one of mine. Maybe I sneezed on you.'

'No,' said Marcus. 'You didn't sneeze on me. It was my idea.'

'Well, can I try it too?' asked Mila.

'Of course!' said Marcus.

Mila jumped from her bed to Marcus's bed. She dropped down to the chest of drawers, and stepped across the bookshelf. She leapt from the bookshelf to the mini-trampoline, then swung on the light cord.

Soon, there were two Tinkler children hanging from the doorframe.

'That was so cool,' said Mila. 'Let's keep going. Should we try to make it all the way to the kitchen?'

Marcus smiled. This was definitely one of Mila's good ideas.

CHAPTER TWO

MARCUS AND MILA swung from the doorframe onto their rocket ship made of ice-cream sticks in the hallway.

From there they leapt onto an upside-down metal pot. From the pot they hopped onto the rabbit hutch. From the rabbit hutch they climbed onto a crate full of Turtle's sticks. Then they jumped up and caught hold of a model solar

17

system hanging from the ceiling, and swung over to a lump of space rock, which they had carried home from the park the week before. From the space rock it was easy to hop onto the kitchen table.

Turtle was under the table, eating a lettuce. 'Mine,' said Turtle, growling. Then she tilted her head to one side. 'Did you know that lettuce belongs to the sunflower family?'

Marcus was never sure if Turtle was very smart for a little kid or very not-smart for a little kid. Maybe she was both.

'I didn't know that,' said Mila. She turned to Marcus. 'It's your turn to get the cake down from the top shelf.'

It was Saturday, and the Tinklers knew:

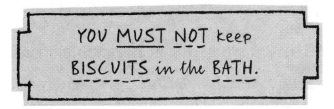

You **MUST** eat cake on **SATURDAYS!**

Even though the Tinklers Three lived alone, they knew that it was important to have rules. Luckily, Mila knew lots of rules. She knew:

YOU **MUST NOT** keep **BISCUITS** in the **BATH**.

She knew:

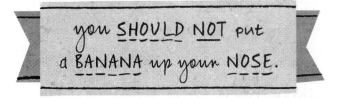

you **SHOULD NOT** put a **BANANA** up your **NOSE**.

She knew:

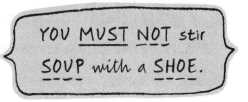

YOU **MUST NOT** stir **SOUP** with a **SHOE**.

Sometimes Marcus wondered if Mila had the rules quite right. Sometimes he thought she just made them up.

But they all agreed on one rule:

BREAKABLE things must be kept on the TOP SHELF in the KITCHEN.

This was because breakable things make a much louder noise when they fall from up high. Bad-for-you food was kept up there too. This was because bad-for-you food tastes even better when you have to climb up high to get it.

When the Tinklers didn't feel like climbing up the shelves they used their special grabby hand. Are you wondering what a grabby hand is?

It's a long stick with a grabber on the end. It is very useful for getting things down from high places. It is also very useful for feeding bread to birds as they fly past the window, for drawing on the ceiling, and for squeezing the noses of people from far away. The grabby hand was one of Marcus's inventions.

Today Marcus didn't use the grabby hand. Today Marcus felt like climbing. He got the cake and climbed back down onto the table.

Mila had a dreamy look on her face.

'What are you thinking about?' asked Marcus.

'I'm thinking about how fun it is not touching the ground,' said Mila. 'Do you think you could make it to the front door of our flat?'

'No problem,' said Marcus. He knew that would be easy.

'So could I,' said Mila. 'What about to the ground floor of our building? Could you make it that far?'

'Yep,' said Marcus.

'I could too,' said Mila. 'And could you go all the way to the corner of our block?'

'Of course!' said Marcus. 'And so could you. We're circus children, don't forget.'

Secretly, Marcus was not so sure they really *could* do it. But he was not going to tell Mila that.

'I am not a circus child,' said Turtle from under the table. 'I am a circus turtle.'

But Marcus and Mila didn't hear her. They were busy thinking.

Marcus looked out the window. From the kitchen, he could see right across the city. He could see all the buildings and television antennas and chimney pots. And far, far off in the distance he could see the city's clock tower.

'I bet I could make it all the way to that clock tower,' he said. 'By dinner time.'

Mila jumped up. She forgot she was standing on the table and put her foot right in the cake. But she didn't notice.

'Me too!' she shouted. 'I could get across the WHOLE CITY without once touching the ground.'

'It won't be easy,' said Marcus slowly.

'No, it won't,' agreed Mila.

'It will probably be dangerous,' said Marcus.

'Very dangerous,' said Mila.

'And we will probably get dirty,' said Marcus.

'Yes,' said Mila. 'Dirtier than we have ever been before.'

Marcus shrugged. 'Well, I guess that decides it then.'

Mila nodded. 'Exactly! Let's go right now!'

CHAPTER THREE

MARCUS AND MILA got dressed. They combed most of their hair and brushed almost all their teeth. They packed their backpacks full of useful things. They did all this without once touching the ground. Then they met up by the front door.

'Right,' said Mila. 'Let's go!'

'Hang on,' said Marcus. 'What about Turtle?'

Turtle was still under the kitchen table eating lettuce.

'You'll have to carry her,' said Mila.

'Me?' said Marcus. 'Why me?'

'Because it's Saturday,' Mila shrugged. Mila said the rule was:

On Saturdays, Marcus MUST carry Turtle.

Marcus had never heard this rule before. He wasn't even sure that it was Saturday. But he was keen to start their mission.

'Maybe we can take it in turns,' said Marcus.

'Maybe,' said Mila.

Marcus grabbed the can of circus glue that his mum had sent him. She used it to stick herself to the horses.

Marcus sprayed the glue all over Turtle.
He didn't want to drop her.

The Tinklers' building had a lift, but
today it was broken. 'Uh-oh,' said
Marcus. 'How do we get downstairs
without touching the ground?'

'We can slide down the banister,' said
Mila.

'Of course!' said Marcus. 'Why didn't I
think of that?'

'There's just one problem,' said Mila.
'How do we get across to the banister
from here?'

Marcus and Mila were standing on a
giant pumpkin near the front door. The
banister was too far away to jump to.

Marcus opened his backpack. Right at the top were two pairs of stilts. He had made them from empty tin cans.

'Great idea!' said Mila. 'We can use those to walk without touching the ground. Why didn't I think of that?'

It is hard to walk on stilts. But it is even harder when your sister who thinks she is a turtle is sitting on your shoulders.

CLUMP. CLUMP. CLUMP.

31

Finally they reached the banister. Now came the fun part!

The banisters in the Tinklers' building were very wide, very smooth and very twisty. In other words, they were PERFECT for sliding down.

WHOOSH!

Mila slid down first, and Marcus
followed close behind, with Turtle
on his shoulders.

On the floor below the Tinklers lived grumpy old Mrs Fitz.

'Slow down!' she yelled, but she was smiling as the Tinklers **WHOOSHED** past.

To tell you the truth, Mrs Fitz was not really grumpy. She was not even very old.

But the Tinklers knew that it was important to have a grumpy adult living nearby, so they asked Mrs Fitz to pretend to be cross with them.

To keep the Tinklers happy, Mrs Fitz banged loudly on the ceiling of her flat with her broom at least twice a day.

She huffed crossly at the Tinkler children whenever she met them on the stairs. And every Sunday the Tinklers went down to her flat so she could give them a good ticking-off.

The Tinklers knew that children needed a good ticking-off once a week, and Mrs Fitz said she didn't mind doing it. Afterwards they would all eat cake together.

But today there was no time to stop and chat with Mrs Fitz. There was no time to be ticked off or eat cake. The Tinklers were on a mission!

CHAPTER FOUR

SO FAR, everything was going well. Very well. And then the Tinklers slid down to the level where the Splatley family lived.

In the Splatley family there was Mr Splatley, Mrs Splatley and their three children: Sarah, Simon and Susie. Sarah Splatley was the same age as Mila.

Simon Splatley was the same age as Marcus. And Susie Splatley was the same age as Turtle.

It is lovely to have fun and friendly children living in the same building as you. But the Splatley children were not fun and friendly. The Splatley children were absolutely AWFUL.

Here are some of the things the Splatley children liked to do:

Pinch babies.

SMACK PUPPIES.

Cut off girls' ponytails.

Spy on their neighbours.

Most of the time their faces were all scrunched up like paper bags. The only time they smiled was when they saw someone getting into trouble.

See how awful they were?

As well as being awful, the Splatleys were terrible stickybeaks, so the Tinklers always tried to go past the Splatleys' floor without making a sound.

Maybe they won't hear us, thought Marcus. *We are sliding very quietly.*

But just as the Tinklers got close to the Splatleys' front door, it sprang wide open. Mr and Mrs Splatley leapt out. Their children stood behind them.

'WHAT are you doing?' boomed Mrs Splatley.

'Get off that banister at once!' squeaked Mr Splatley. 'You'll fall.'

'We won't fall,' Marcus told them. 'We have circus blood.'

The Splatley children smiled, but not in a nice way.

'You're in trouble!' Sarah said in a sing-song voice.

'BIG trouble,' giggled Simon.

Susie just stuck out her tongue.

'Why don't you three come inside?' said Mr Splatley. 'We're playing Ludo.'

Marcus opened his mouth to say no. Firstly, the Tinklers were on a mission. And secondly, playing Ludo with the Splatleys did not sound like fun.

But before Marcus could say no, Mila sneezed.

Phew! thought Marcus. *Mila must have an idea.*

So he was very surprised when Mila said, 'We would LOVE to play Ludo!'

What was going on?

'Well, come inside then,' said Mrs Splatley.

But Mila shook her head. 'First I need a tray. A big one, please.'

'What for?' asked Mrs Splatley.

'We have our own special way of playing Ludo,' said Mila. 'I'll show you.'

Then she winked at Marcus.

Ah, thought Marcus. *Mila has a plan after all.*

Mr Splatley went and got a tray. It was a nice big metal one.

'Perfect!' said Mila. 'Now, can you please put it on the ground?'

Mr Splatley put the tray on the ground. 'This is a very unusual way to play Ludo,' he said.

'Yes,' said Mila. 'It is very unusual. But it's the best way.'

Mila looked at Marcus. She spoke to him in a very quiet voice. 'When I count to three, jump from the banister onto the tray. OK?'

Marcus nodded.

'One, two, three – JUMP!'

Mila jumped onto the tray, then Marcus hopped on behind her, with Turtle still balancing on his shoulders. The tray began to slide down the stairs. Most children would fall off. But the Tinklers didn't even wobble.

'Stop!' boomed Mrs Splatley as the tray zoomed off down the stairs. 'That is NOT how you play Ludo!'

But the Tinklers Three did not stop. They **WHOOSHED** down and down, around and around.

'You told a lie to the Splatleys,' Marcus said to Mila as they whooshed along. 'Isn't it wrong to lie?'

'Oh no,' said Mila. 'It's fine to lie when it's about playing Ludo with the Splatleys.'

Marcus was just thinking what a good rule this was when they crashed into a wall on the third floor.

The Tinklers Three did not fall off the tray. Not even one finger or toe touched the ground.

But the tray was now very bent.

'It's too bent to ride anymore,' said Marcus. 'What do we do next?'

The clock tower was a long way away. And they were not getting any closer to it.

'We go out there,' said Mila. She pointed to a window in the stairwell.

CHAPTER Five

ON THE OTHER SIDE of the window was a very tall tree. The Tinklers Three often climbed it. But they had never climbed it by going out the window. Marcus got his tin-can stilts out again and clumped across to the window. Mila clumped up beside him. They looked out at the tree.

'If we climb to the top we can get onto

the roof of that building,' Mila said, pointing to a building just behind the tree. 'Then we will be well on our way.'

'But how do we get to the tree?' asked Marcus.

'What about if we use this?' said Mila. Out of her backpack she pulled a bow and arrow with a rope attached to the end. This was something Marcus had invented to collect the Tinklers' mail. The postman just needed to stand on the street holding out the letters. Then Marcus could shoot an arrow out the window, hit the letters and pull them back up to the thirty-third floor. (But, so far, the postman had not agreed to this.)

'We can shoot the arrow across to the tree and then walk across the rope.

Just pretend the rope is a tightrope,' said Mila. 'Unless you're too scared?'

Marcus shook his head. 'Of course I'm not too scared!' he said. 'I'm a Tinkler, after all.'

Here is a secret: Marcus WAS scared.

But he was not going to tell Mila that!

Mila aimed at the tree. She drew back the bow and . . .

TWANG!

The arrow flew through the air.

The rope curled around and around one of the tree's branches.

Then Mila pulled it tight. 'Now for the easy part,' she said. 'We just have to walk across the rope.'

Marcus watched Mila walk across. It didn't look easy to him. It looked very scary. Sometimes Marcus wondered if he had less circus blood than Mila did.

'I don't think I should do that,' said Marcus. 'Turtle is scared.'

'No, I'm not,' said Turtle. 'It will be fun. We'll be like monkeys in the jungle.'

'You're a turtle, not a monkey,' said Marcus.

'You are scared,' said Turtle. 'Here. I will spray the rope with circus glue.' She got out the can of glue and sprayed it. But she missed the rope and got the windowsill instead.

'Don't do that, Turtle,' said Marcus. 'You're wasting the glue. And you are making the windowsill super sticky.'

Just then there was a noise on the stairs. Someone was coming down. Marcus heard a laugh. It sounded like chickens gargling. Only three people in the world could make a laugh sound so bad. THE SPLATLEY THREE!

'Marcus,' said Turtle. 'What is more scary? Walking on that rope or getting stuck here with the Spatleys?'

'You're right,' said Marcus. 'Let's go.'

So Marcus carefully stepped over the sticky patch on the windowsill and started to walk across the tightrope.

Marcus was halfway across when he heard the sound of **chickens gargling** again. This time it was much louder.

It is very difficult to turn around on a tightrope, but Marcus needed to see what was going on. And it was just as well that he did!

The Splatley children were leaning out the window. Sarah was holding a big pair of **SCISSORS**.

'It's naughty to walk on tightropes!' called Simon.

'So we're going to cut the rope,' said Sarah.

Susie stuck out her tongue.

That tongue gave Marcus an idea. 'Did you know,' he said to the Splatleys, 'that this windowsill is made of sugar?'

'Don't be dumb,' said Sarah. 'That's not true.'

'Oh really?' said Marcus. 'Then why don't you try it? Then you can prove me wrong.'

The Splatley children loved nothing more than proving someone wrong. They all stuck out their tongues and licked the windowsill together.

Of course, it is a very silly idea to lick a windowsill at any time. But it is even sillier when the windowsill has been sprayed with circus glue. Soon all three Splatleys had their tongues stuck to the windowsill.

'Helth!' cried Sarah.

'We'll thee thtuck here thorether!' Simon said.

'Not forever,' said Marcus. 'Circus glue wears off after a few hours.'

'What a pity,' sighed Turtle.

Suddenly Marcus wasn't scared any more. He was sure he had lots of circus blood. Only a true circus kid could trick those Splatleys so easily! Marcus turned around on the tightrope and ran carefully across to the tree, with Turtle clinging to his neck.

CHAPTER SIX

'IT IS YOUR TURN to carry Turtle,' said Marcus to Mila once he was in the tree.

'Look, I would love to,' said Mila. 'But I can't.'

'Why not?'

'It's against the rules, remember?' said Mila. 'Sorry.'

She started climbing up the tree before Marcus could argue.

So Marcus climbed up the tree with Turtle on his shoulders. All the Tinklers could climb very well. Even Turtle, when she was not being a turtle.

But this was a very big tree.

It went up and UP and UP and UP.

As they climbed, the tree trunk got narrower. Then it began to lean to one side. The higher the Tinklers climbed, the more the tree leaned. Finally the Tinklers ran out of tree to climb. But by now the tree had bent so much that it was touching the roof of the next building.

'Oh good,' said Mila. 'Now we can easily get onto that building.' She started to step across onto the roof.

'Stop!' cried Marcus. 'If you step onto the roof and let go of the tree, the tree will spring back, and Turtle and I will go flying!'

'Oh. Good point,' said Mila. 'I'll hold onto the top of the tree until you and Turtle are safely on the roof.'

'Well, OK . . .' said Marcus slowly.

The problem was that sometimes Mila forgot what she was supposed to be doing. She would go out to buy oranges and come back three hours later with an orangutan instead.

Marcus hoped she would not forget the plan right now. He did not want to go flying across the sky like a stone from a slingshot!

But luckily Mila did not forget.

She climbed onto the roof and held on tight to the top of the tree so it didn't spring back. Marcus climbed across and looked around him.

Everywhere he looked he could see rooftops. They looked like the squares of a patchwork blanket. And in the distance he could see the clock tower. Some of the roofs were bare. Some of them had gardens. A few of them had swimming pools.

The best bit was that most of the roofs were very close together. So close that Marcus and Mila could jump from one building to the next. Of course, most children would not be able to do this. It was only possible because circus children have extra-springy feet and no-one to tell them off.

The Tinklers Three ran and jumped from one roof to another. They ran around chimneys and satellite dishes.

They ran through rooftop gardens. And when they needed to cool down they swam through swimming pools. They ran and they jumped until Turtle said she was hungry.

'Me too,' said Marcus. 'Let's have lunch.'

Mila and Marcus looked in their bags. 'What about an apple?' said Mila. 'Or a tomato sandwich?'

'No,' said Turtle. 'I want lettuce.'

'What about some salami?' Marcus suggested. 'Or some yak cheese? Or a seagull egg? Hard-boiled of course.'

'No,' said Turtle. 'No, no, NO! I want lettuce!'

Mila and Marcus looked at each other. 'We will have to get her one somehow,' said Mila.

'Yes,' agreed Marcus. 'If we want to finish our mission.'

Mila walked over to the edge of the building and looked down below. 'Hey!' she said. 'I can see someone's vegetable garden. There are rows and rows of lettuces.'

Marcus frowned. 'If we go down there we will touch the ground,' he said. 'Then we'll have failed our mission.' Marcus thought for a moment. 'How about we use the grabby hand?' he said. 'I brought it with me.'

This was another reason why the Tinklers were lucky to live alone. Adults would have told Marcus it was useless to bring the grabby hand. But the Tinklers Three knew that a grabby hand was always useful.

CHAPTER SEVEN

MARCUS LEANT over the edge of the roof. He stretched out the grabby hand as far as it would go. But looking down below made his head spin. He shut his eyes. That stopped him feeling dizzy. He moved the grabby hand around until it grabbed onto something. Then he lifted it up.

Mila and Marcus and Turtle looked at the thing Marcus had grabbed.

'That is not a lettuce,' said Turtle. 'That is a carrot.'

'Oops,' said Marcus. He leant back over the edge and put the carrot back in the ground. Then he tried again.

'That's also not a lettuce,' said Mila when she saw what he had grabbed this time. 'That's a cat.'

The cat did not look happy.

Turtle didn't look happy either. 'Where is my lettuce?' she asked.

'Here. Let me do it,' said Mila.

She took the grabby hand from Marcus and leant over the edge. A moment later she pulled up a lettuce. Turtle ate it.

'Another one, please,' she said.

So Mila pulled up another lettuce for Turtle. Then another one.

'There are a lot of holes in that vegie patch now,' Mila said. 'The gardener might be upset.'

'How about we put some of our things in the holes as payment?' said Marcus.

Mila nodded. 'That's only fair.' She picked up the salami and planted it in one of the holes. She planted the sandwich in another. The third hole she filled with the seagull egg. 'Maybe they will grow,' she said. 'Maybe the salami will turn into a salami tree.'

'Maybe,' said Marcus. But he didn't really think that would happen.

After lunch the Tinklers were full of energy. They ran even faster and jumped even further. Marcus didn't feel like he was even running anymore. He felt like he was ⹀FLYING. The clock tower got closer and closer.

'We're going to do it!' Mila shouted happily. 'We're going to make it to the clock tower by dinner time.'

By now they were in the very fancy part of town. Some of the roofs had playgrounds, and one even had a big trampoline! Of course the Tinklers Three could never pass a trampoline without trying it out. And this one was a very springy trampoline. So springy that the Tinklers could use it to jump across two rooftops in one go!

'Look!' said Marcus when he landed. 'We're almost there.'

This was true. There were no more rooftops to run over. No more chimneys. No more satellite dishes. The clock tower was right in front of them.

The only problem was that there was a very big gap between the last roof and the clock tower. And it was almost dinner time.

When three children stand at the edge of a building, a lot of people notice. So it wasn't long before a big crowd was gathered, looking up and pointing at them.

'We'll have to hurry,' said Mila. 'An adult might come up and try to stop us from finishing our mission.'

Marcus knew she was right. But he also didn't know what to do.

'Bird!' said Turtle.

She was right. There was a pigeon standing on the edge of the building.

Lots of people don't like pigeons.

They think they are dirty. But the Tinklers liked them. Marcus liked feeding them bits of seed bread out of the window. Mila liked wearing their nests as hats.

'Maybe that bird will fly us across to the clock tower,' said Mila. 'If we ask it politely.'

Now, of course, most people know that you can't talk to birds. But no-one had ever told the Tinklers this.

Marcus nodded. 'That's a good idea.' He turned to the pigeon. 'Excuse me, bird. Could you fly us over to the clock tower? If we don't get there in ten minutes we'll fail our mission.'

Most birds would just fly off if a kid asked them something as crazy as this.

But this pigeon knew the Tinklers. It often flew past when Marcus was handing out seed bread with the grabby hand. In fact most of the pigeons in the city knew the Tinklers.

Unfortunately, this pigeon had plans for that afternoon. First he was going to fly to a park and sit on the head of a sculpture. Then he was going to poo on someone's clean washing. He didn't really have time to help the Tinklers.

But then the bird thought about the tasty seed bread. Pigeons like eating seed bread even more than they like pooing on clean washing.

Here is what that bird thought:

Coo...coo... If I don't help the Tinklers, maybe they won't feed us anymore!

The bird flew off.

'Oh no!' said Marcus.

'Now we won't be able to finish our mission,' sighed Mila.

But she was wrong.

CHAPTER Eight

BY NOW, most of the people in the city were on the ground, looking up at the Tinklers. There were fire engines and police cars. There were people with nets and people with megaphones shouting things. But they were all calling out at the same time, so all the Tinklers could hear was: 'BLRRGRBH! SHIRIFSBST! ZZT!'

Marcus looked down. 'Maybe we could jump down onto those nets,' he said. 'We might bounce back up to the clock tower.'

'That could work,' said Mila. 'Or maybe we could wait for a cloud to come past. Then we could float to the clock tower on that.'

'That could work too,' said Marcus. 'But there are no clouds today.'

'Bird!' said Turtle again.

But what she should have said was 'birds', because not only had the pigeon come back but he had brought friends. *Hundreds* of friends, in fact. He had flown around telling the other pigeons that the Tinkler children needed their help. He'd pointed out that if they didn't help there might not be any more seed bread for them.

All the pigeons in the city flew to where the Tinkler children were standing. And they did something very strange: They clumped together into the shape of a giant bird. A *fluttering,* flapping, giant bird.

The Tinklers looked at the giant bird.

'I think,' said Marcus slowly, 'that they want us to climb onto their backs.'

Mila nodded. 'Yes, that's exactly what they want.'

So that is what the Tinklers Three did.

Flying on a giant bird made from smaller birds is not easy. It is even harder when there is a wind blowing and you are up very high and you are carrying your little sister on your shoulders. But the Tinklers, as you know, are circus children, so they had no problems at all.

The giant bird flew across to the top of the clock tower just as the clock struck six o'clock. Dinner time.

The crowd down below had gone very quiet while all this was going on.

But once the Tinklers were safely on the tower, everyone on the ground began to cheer and clap. This was because they were glad the children weren't hurt. It was also because it had been very exciting to watch them flying on the giant bird.

The Tinklers didn't hear the people cheering. All they heard were the pigeons who had started cooing loudly.

This is what the pigeons were saying:

You Tinklers better give us EXTRA seed bread tomorrow!

Coo...coo...

And then the pigeons split up and flew away.

'Well,' said Mila. 'What should we do now?'

'Now we should go home,' said Marcus.

'Back the same way we came?' asked Mila.

Marcus shook his head. 'No. Let's catch the underground train.' He unstuck Turtle from his shoulders and handed her to Mila.

'What are you doing?' asked Mila.

'This is one of our rules, don't you remember?' said Marcus. 'If I carry Turtle $OVER$ the city, you must carry her $UNDER$ it!'

★　★　★

INTRODUCING
the TINKLERS THREE

MARCUS

Age: Eight.

How to spot him: He's the kid who is always collecting things to use in his inventions.

Favourite place to escape: His workshop in the basement.

Hobbies: Reading comics, swimming, going to the pet park, inventing things.

Biggest dream: He'd like to invent the world's best mailbox.

Dislikes: Adults who think the Tinklers need a grown-up to look after them.

Favourite food: Cheese and pineapple pancakes (he invented these himself!).

Biggest secret: He isn't sure he wants to join the circus like his parents. He thinks he might like to be an inventor instead.

MILA

<u>Age</u>: Ten.

<u>How to spot her</u>: She's the girl with a bird's nest on her head.

<u>Likes</u>: Making up new rules.

<u>Dislikes</u>: Playing Ludo with the Splatley family.

<u>Biggest dream</u>: To make a bed she could wear so she would never have to get up.

<u>Thing that annoys her most</u>: Ice-cream should come in bigger tubs (bathtub size would be perfect!).

<u>Current project</u>: Doing special arm exercises so she can learn to fly.

<u>When she grows up</u>: Mila can't wait to join the circus like her parents.

<u>Favourite thing to cook</u>: Upside-down cake. She makes it while hanging upside down.

TURTLE

Age: Three.

How to spot her: She's the kid with a box tied to her back.

Why is she called Turtle? Because she thinks she is one.

Favourite book: *Big Book of Turtle Facts* (written by Mila Tinkler).

Favourite food: Something that starts with 'L' and ends with 'ettuce'.

Favourite things to play with: Boxes and sticks.

She is smart because: She already knows how to read and uses lots of big words.

She is not so smart because: She thinks turtles can growl and fetch sticks.

When she grows up: She wants to be a shark.

THE SPLATLEYS

SARAH

<u>Ages</u>: Ten (Sarah), eight (Simon), and three (Susie).

<u>How to spot them</u>: They are the ones doing something horrible.

<u>Hobbies</u>: Being sneaky and mean. Getting other people into trouble. Laughing when other people hurt themselves. Playing Ludo.

<u>Favourite food</u>: Anything they've snatched out of someone else's hand.

SIMON

SUSIE

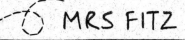

MRS FITZ

<u>Age</u>: She pretends to be eighty but she is really only sixty.

<u>How to spot her</u>: She is the lady who is always trying to look grumpy.

<u>Hobbies</u>: Making soup, banging on the ceiling with a broom, and disco dancing.

<u>On Sundays</u>: She gives the Tinklers Three a good ticking-off and then she gives them cake.

<u>Something the Tinklers don't know</u>: Mrs Fitz keeps an eye on the Tinklers Three, but she makes sure they don't know she's doing it!

<u>Secret dream</u>: Mrs Fitz would love to join the circus one day.

THE TINKLERS THREE

THREE GREAT ADVENTURES!

a VERY good IDEA

M·C·BADGER

AN excellent INVENTION

M·C·BADGER

the coolest POOL

M·C·BADGER